For my mom and dad, Bruce and Esther Caplan,
who always encourage me to make my dreams take flight!
—B.C.S.

To Annie
—C.S.

Text copyright © 2017 by Brianna Caplan Sayres
Jacket art and interior illustrations copyright © 2017 by Christian Slade

Random House and the colophon are registered trademarks of Penguin Random House LLC.

Visit us on the Web! randomhousekids.com

Educators and librarians, for a variety of teaching tools, visit us at RHTeachersLibrarians.com

Library of Congress Cataloging-in-Publication Data
Names: Sayres, Brianna Caplan, author. | Slade, Christian, illustrator.
Title: Where do jet planes sleep at night? / Brianna Caplan Sayres, Christian Slade.
Description: First Edition. | New York : Random House, [2017] |
Summary: Illustrations and rhyming text reveal what airplanes, helicopters,
and blimps do to get ready for bed after a hard day's work.
Identifiers: LCCN 2015043999 | ISBN 978-0-399-55448-3 (trade) |
ISBN 978-0-399-55449-0 (lib. bdg.) | ISBN 978-0-399-55450-6 (ebook)
Subjects: | CYAC: Stories in rhyme. | Airplanes—Fiction. | Helicopters—Fiction. | Airships—Fiction. | Bedtime—Fiction.
Classification: LCC PZ8.3.S274 Whg 2017 | DDC [E]—dc23

MANUFACTURED IN CHINA
10 9 8 7 6 5 4 3 2 1
First Edition

Where Do Jet Planes Sleep at Night?

by Brianna Caplan Sayres · illustrated by Christian Slade

Random House New York

Where do jet planes sleep at night
after a day of engines roaring?
Do dads share bedtime tales
of their transatlantic soaring?

Where do biplanes sleep at night—
those planes from long ago?
Do moms say, "Stop your stunts, kids!
Tomorrow's another show"?

Where do helicopters sleep,
since they rise straight up in the air?
Do dads say, "No more hovering,"
as kids twirl their teddy bear?

Where do skywriting planes sleep
after writing way up high?
Do moms read them bedtime stories
that are written in the sky?

Where do hang gliders sleep at night
after a day filled up with soaring?
Does flying without engines
leave them super tired and snoring?

Where do hot-air balloons sleep
after flames have made them rise?
Do they float off into dreamland
as the sunset fills the skies?

Where do supersonic planes sleep
after a day of endless rushing?
Does super-speed help clean their teeth
with aeronautic brushing?

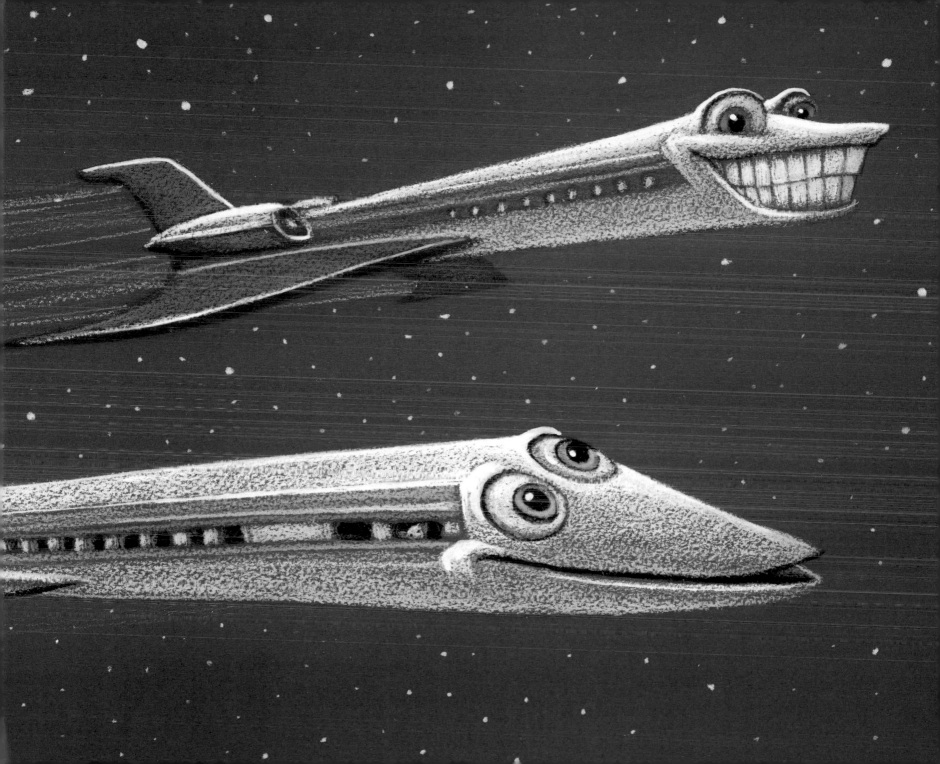

Where do giant blimps sleep
after floating overhead?
Do they leave that noisy stadium
for a quiet flower bed?

Where does Air Force One sleep
after traveling far and wide?
Does the White House plane dream about
its next presidential ride?

Where do seaplanes sleep at night
after they land on their pontoons?
Do lakes become their bathtubs
beneath a glowing moon?

Where do all these aircraft sleep
once they've gone up and come back down?
Do they get cozy on a runway
or a field outside of town?

Do they hug plane moms with their wings?
Is the tower their night-light?
They dream of takeoffs and landings
and of lovely views in flight!

Where do your planes sleep at night
when it's time for you to sleep?
They help you off to dreamland,
counting planes instead of sheep!